Michael Makes Maps

PAGE PUBLISHING, INC.
Conneaut Lake, PA

First originally published by Page Publishing 2020

ISBN 978-1-64584-916-2 (pbk)
ISBN 978-1-64584-917-9 (digital)

Printed in the United States of America

Michael Makes Maps

Cheryl Womack-Whye

1

After school on Friday, Michael burst into his father's study. "Hey, Dad! I made a great map! I'm a cartographer just like you." Michael's loose dark curls danced as he hopped.

"Uh-huh." No smile. Dad's brown hands kept moving across his drafting table.

Michael looked at the picture of Mom's creamy skin and bright smile. Her memorial had been at the end of winter, but Dad still seemed frozen in sadness.

Michael grabbed his pencils, pens, markers, and lots of paper. "My maps will make you smile!" He dashed out the back-screen door and made maps of every part of his green sunny yard and his woods.

Michael showed all of these to Dad. "This one's a treasure map. Don't you want to go to the big red X? I bet Mom would."

"Not now," Dad whispered.

"Adventures made Mom smile." Michael leaned against Dad. "We always had fun in the woods."

Dad looked down and patted Michael's shoulder. "I'll go after I finish my work."

"You never finish." Michael scrunched up his face and stomped off. "I'll make a map for my best friend."

Saturday afternoon, Michael called out, "Semira, I made a great map for you."

She zipped over and studied the map. "What's at the big red X?"

Michael grinned. "It's something special."

Semira smiled. "Ooh, I'm going to find it!" She ran through his yard and through his woods until…*KER-SMUSH*! "Gross! Mud and slime and DEAD BUGS. YECH! MICHAEL!! This is not a nice map. You are not a nice friend!"

Semira stomped back through the woods, the yard, and into Michael's house, leaving a muddy slimy trail.

Dad stood next to Michael.

Semira opened the front door, scrunched up her face, plucked an almost-dead bug from her light-brown hair and said, "Michael is mean!"

Dad studied the map. His eyebrows made one dark line. "Would Mom have liked this map?"

"It's a great map…but I guess not." He looked at the floor. "I just miss Mom."

"I do too." Dad bear-hugged Michael. "Please clean this up and get ready for bed."

As Michael scooched deep between his covers, he said, "I miss Mom's smile."

"So do I." Dad tucked him in. "No more maps until you can make one that would make her smile. And no more visits from Semira."

Michael buried his face in his pillow, so Dad wouldn't hear. "You're mean."

Monday morning, Semira didn't smile at Michael. She held onto their favorite ball and went to play with other children.

"You're being mean," Michael shouted and stomped away right into the biggest puddle on the playground. *KER-SPLASH*! Drops flew everywhere, and muddy water filled his shoes. "Oh, gross!" He sat down to shake out his shoes, and the water on the bench wet his pants.

Some of the children laughed and pointed. His best friend just looked sad.

Michael felt so sad that he didn't move when the bell rang. He didn't even move when his teacher called him, so she called his father.

Soon Dad opened the school door. "Come on in, Michael." Dad gave him a little hug and some dry clothes. "What happened?"

"Semira was mean to me. She didn't even talk to me. I didn't have any fun."

"Hm. Do you think *she* had fun last weekend?"

Michael looked at the floor. "I guess. Maybe not."

"I'm sorry you didn't have fun today." Dad gave Michael a bigger hug. "I've got to go back to work. Hm. I wonder what Mom would do?"

Michael sat and thought. Then he whispered to Semira, "I'm sorry you didn't have fun at my house."

The next day, Michael brought in a map and showed it to his teacher. She smiled just like Mom and said, "Class, Michael made a map for us."

He gave the map to Semira. "There really is something *special* at the big red X."

Semira looked at the teacher's smile. She studied Michael's map for a long time, then Semira smiled at her best friend.

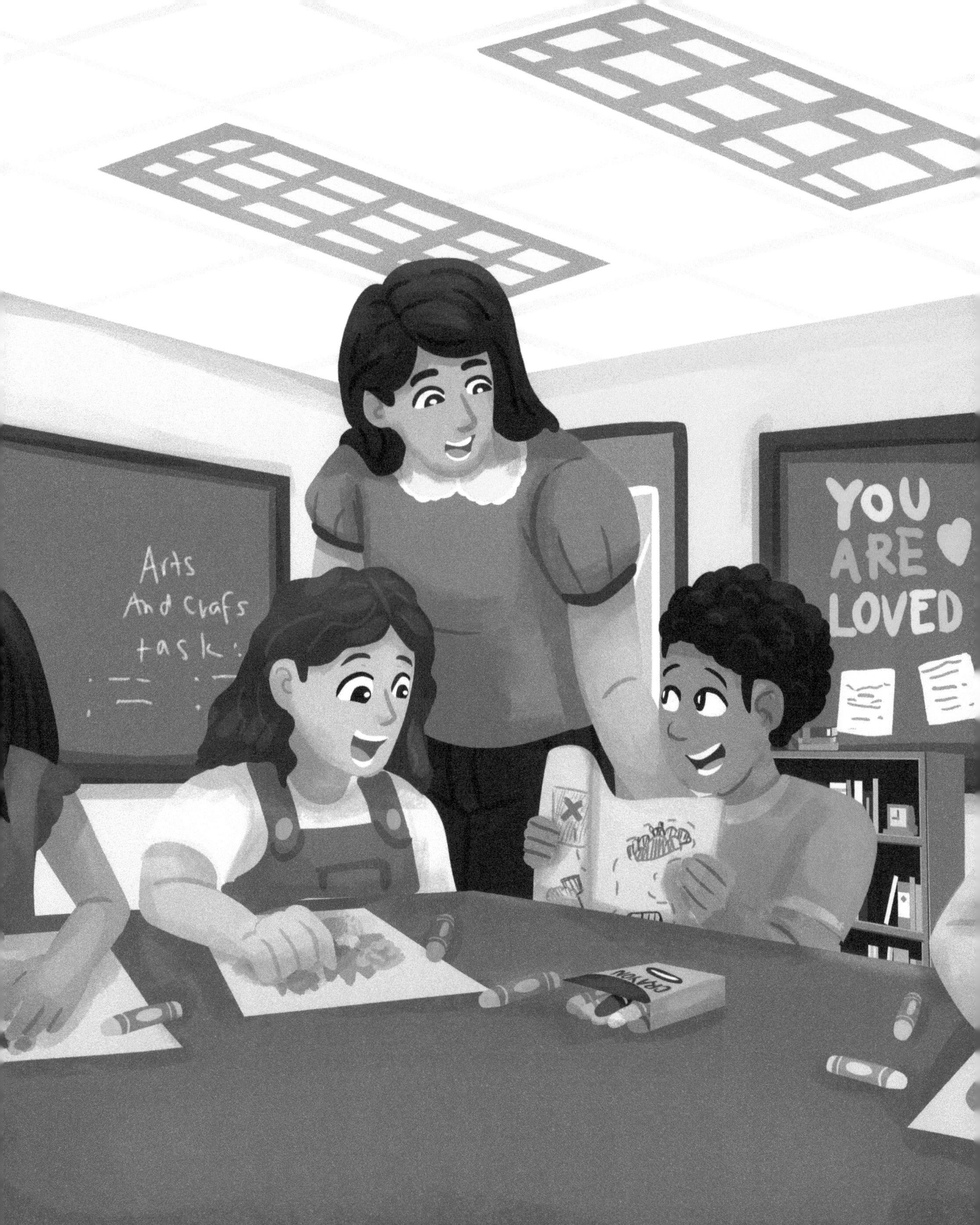
Arts
And Crafs
task :
YOU
ARE
LOVED
CRAYON

Just before lunch, Michael's dad joined the class as Semira led everyone past the art room door, into the library, around the bookcase of outer space stories, and back into the hallway. Finally, she led everyone into the cafeteria. A big red X was on their table. On the X was a huge pile of cupcakes.

They all smiled and cheered, "Michael, you made a great map!"

Dad's smile was the biggest.

ABOUT THE AUTHOR

Cheryl Womack-Whye is a forever teacher and learner who is a passionate proponent for the synergy of knowledge that occurs at every phase from birth to adult. Her mother, also an educator, developed Cheryl's map-reading skills during their adventurous car trips throughout many states. While her brother just played in the backseat, she would sit in the navigator's seat with a pencil and trace the path from here to there, finding shortcuts and ways around traffic jams. Cheryl's three children grew to have the same love of maps and often use them when traveling and exploring new places. Cheryl laughs at the fact that without a map, she'd get lost going around the corner, so she takes a map and frequently a friend along on her adventures in her new home state of Delaware.

CPSIA information can be obtained
at www.ICGtesting.com
Printed in the USA
BVHW091304190520
579966BV00011B/221

9 781645 849162